Thomas and the Bees

Learn to read with Thomas

EGMONT
We bring stories to life

First published in Great Britain 2008
by Egmont UK Limited
239 Kensington High Street, London W8 6SA
All rights reserved.

HiT entertainment

ISBN 978 1 4052 3787 1
1 3 5 7 9 10 8 6 4 2

Printed in Singapore

Learn to read with Thomas

This series of early learning story books draws on the 45 key words that children learn in the first year of the National Curriculum.

The stories contain repetition of these key words and phrases. This will help your child to recognise them, and to make the link between their sounds and their shapes on the page. Your child will also begin to predict what is coming next, thus connecting written and spoken words, enabling them to 'read'.

Listening to stories read aloud motivates children to want to read for themselves, and well-loved characters like Thomas encourage their interest in books.

To get the most out of the stories:

- read them with your child on several occasions;
- use a lively tone of voice and point to the words;
- encourage your child to read aloud the words he/she has learned.

Other activities to enjoy:

- **Follow the train tracks**
  Children can trace with a pencil from left to right in preparation for writing.
- **Find the pictures**
  Children can learn to observe small details in this activity.
- **Spot the difference**
  Children can compare two pictures, a skill used in reading when distinguishing the shapes of letters and words.

Thomas has two coaches called Annie and Clarabel.

He likes them to go as fast as they can.

"You are too slow, Annie," says Thomas. "Faster!"

"I'm going as fast as I can!" says Annie.

"Hurry, Clarabel!" says Thomas. "Faster, faster!"

"I'm going as fast as I can!" says Clarabel.

Some bees fly near Annie and Clarabel.

"Buzz, buzz," say the bees. "Hello."

"I do not like bees," says Annie.

"I do not like bees," says Clarabel.

Annie and Clarabel try to get away from the bees.

They go as fast as they can.

"You are too slow, Thomas!" says Annie.

"Go faster, Thomas!" says Clarabel.

Thomas goes as fast as he can. Now he is pleased.

"Peep!" he says. "I DO like bees!"

These pictures look the same, but there are 5 differences in picture 2.

2

Can you spot them all?

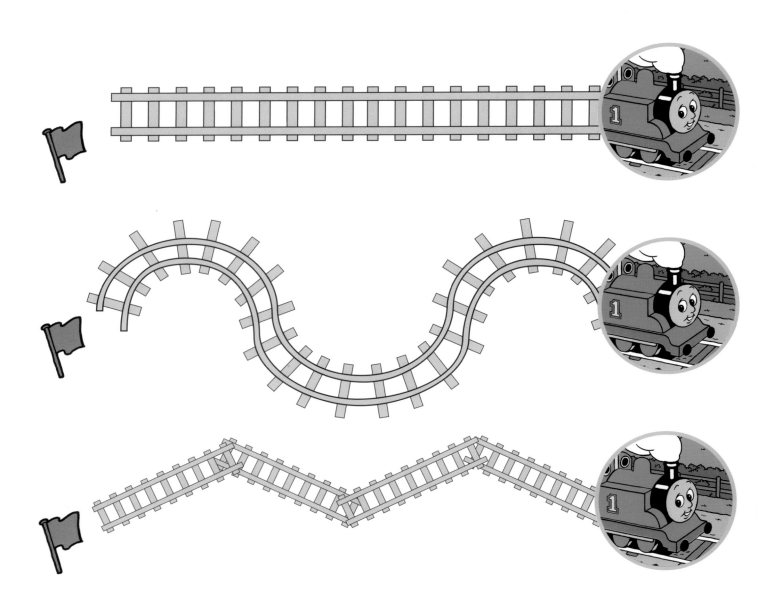

Follow the train tracks with a pencil.
Start at the red flag.

Point to the things in the big picture.

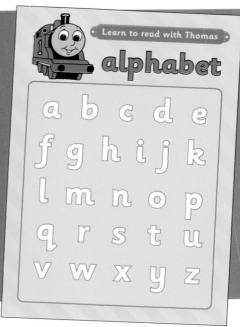

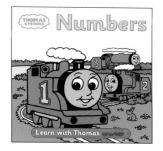

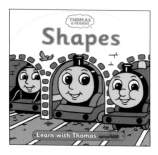
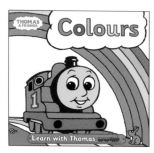

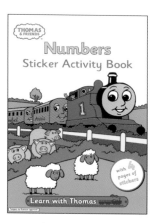
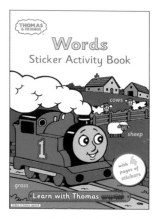